DREAMWORKS
GABBY'S DOLLHOUSE

TREASURE HUNT

Adapted by **GABRIELLE REYES**

SCHOLASTIC INC.

ISBN 978-1-339-01650-4

10 9 8 7 6 5 4 3 2   24 25 26 27 28

Printed the U.S.A.   40

This edition first printing 2024

Book design by **SALENA MAHINA** and **STACIE ZUCKER**

FREE DOWNLOAD
TÉLÉCHARGEMENT GRATUIT

Download on the
App Store

GET IT ON
Google Play

Télécharger dans l'App Store
Disponible sur Google Play

GabbysDollhouse.spinmaster.com

Hi, I'm Gabby!

Pandy Paws and I are going on a treasure hunt.

We will find three charms for my bracelet.

Come help us!

We have a map.

It is a clue.

Where is the first treasure?

The beach!

MerCat can take us on her ship.

CatRat is at the beach.

He has a clue.

The treasure is behind a
pink-and-blue sandcastle.

Can you find the pink-and-blue sandcastle?

Pandy Paws found the treasure!

It is a sea-glass kitty charm!

The charm pops on my bracelet!

Where is the second treasure?

Check the map!

The Wild West!

CatRat has a train.

He can take us.

All aboard!

Howdy, DJ Catnip!

Howdy, Baby Box!

They have a clue.

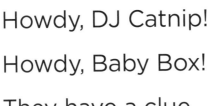

The treasure is under the porch with flowers.

Can you find the porch with flowers?

We found the treasure!

Yeehaw!

It is a gold kitty.

We found two charms!

Where will the third treasure be?

Check the map.

Do you know where to go?

17

The dollhouse kitchen!

Cakey Cat has a clue.

The treasure is inside a cookbook.

Can you find the cookbook?

You found it!

Now, hop in!

It is yummy in here!

Which way is the treasure?

Cakey knows.

The treasure is over the berry bridge.

Look!

This bridge is made of berries.

Let's go!

Cakey has the last clue.

The treasure is in the doughnut tree.

Pandy Paws found it!

25

It is a doughnut kitty!

A-meow-zing!

We found all three charms!

Let's go back to the dollhouse!

I show the Gabby Cats my bracelet.

They helped me find the charms.

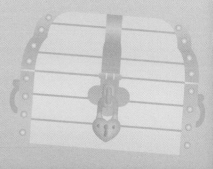

You did, too!

Thanks for joining us!